# MOLLY of DENALI

## Molly's ↓ Awesome Alaska Guide

W9-BJL-518

Special thanks to Rochelle Adams and Dewey Hoffman for their valuable assistance.

MOLLY OF DENALI: Molly's Awesome Alaska Guide
Copyright © 2020 by WGBH Educational Foundation.

PBS KIDS® and the PBS KIDS logo are registered trademarks of Public Broadcasting Service. Used with permission. All rights reserved.
MOLLY OF DENALI™ is a trademark of WGBH Educational Foundation. Used with permission. All rights reserved.

MOLLY OF DENALI™ is produced by WGBH Kids and Atomic Cartoons in association with CBC Kids.

Funding for MOLLY OF DENALI is provided by the Corporation for Public Broadcasting and by public television viewers. In addition, the contents of MOLLY OF DENALI were developed under a grant from the Department of Education. However, those contents do not necessarily represent the policy of the Department of Education, and you should not assume endorsement by the Federal Government. The project is funded by a Ready To Learn grant (PR/AWARD No. U295A150003, CFDA No. 84.295A).

Library of Congress Control Number: 2019950256
ISBN 978-0-06-295042-0

Design by Brenda Echevarrias-Angelilli
19 20 21 22 23 PC/LSCC 10 9 8 7 6 5 4 3 2 1

First Edition

# MOLLY of DENALI

## Molly's ↓ Awesome Alaska Guide

**HARPER**
*An Imprint of* HarperCollins*Publishers*

# Table of Contents

# Greetings from Alaska!

Kotze

Nome

Bethel

Unalaska

Sand Point

Utqiagvik

•Prudhoe Bay

Alaska

Fort Yukon

Fairbanks •

☆Denali

Anchorage
•       •Valdez
Kenai

•Juneau

•Kodiak          Sitka
Juneau is the
capital of Alaska          •Ketchikan

7

# PART 1

# Me, My Friends, and My Family

Hey, I live here!

DENALI

Tooey

Mom—coolest pilot ever!

Trini

I ♥ Dad!

# Hey, everyone, it's me, Molly!

Here I am at the Trading Post.

And this is my guide to life in Qyah (pronounced **KI-yah**), Alaska, where I live. Alaska is the biggest of the 50 states in the United States of America—and Qyah is a village right in the center of it! Qyah is filled with amazing, unique places and animals—not to mention cool people, like my friends—and each day here is an adventure. My guide will tell you everything you want to know about me, my life, and the adventures I go on.

If there are any words in this guide you don't know, check page 62, the glossary!

# Here are some facts about me:

* My full name is Molly Shahnyaa (SHAAH-NYAH) Mabray. Shahnyaa is my Native name. It means "One who informs us" in the Gwich'in language.

* My family is Alaska Native. That means our ancestors have lived in Alaska for thousands of years!

* I like all animals, but I especially like birds, and I ESPECIALLY like puffins!

* I like my dog, Suki, the most of course!

* I live in a store—really! My mom and dad run the Denali Trading Post, and we live upstairs.

Tooey's new sled dog, Anka. She's so smart.

# Meet my friends Tooey . . .

I have been best friends with Tooey since . . . basically forever! My mom, Layla, and his mom, Atsaq, grew up together! Tooey's name is short for "Teekkone," which means "wolf" in Koyukon Athabascan, one of Alaska's many Native languages. Tooey is a lot like a wolf—smart and loyal! Tooey is also great with dogs . . . he's basically a dog whisperer!

"O "O "O "O "O "O "O"

Read more about sled dogs on pages 46–47!

"O "O "O "O "O "O"

# . . . and Trini!

Trini is a new friend. She just moved here from Texas, which is even hotter than Alaska in the summer! I love showing Trini all the cool stuff there is to see and do in Alaska, and Trini loves learning about it. Trini can do anything she puts her mind to. She even won first place in the blanket toss contest this winter at our Fun-Raiser!

# My parents are the BEST!

My mom, Layla, is the best mom a kid could ask for. She's also the bravest person I know—she is a pilot! More specifically, she's a bush pilot—that means she's really good at flying her plane in the Alaskan wilderness, and she can even land the plane without a runway! Mom lets me fly in her plane all the time. We take people where they need to go, bring them supplies—and sometimes we even rescue people when they need help!

My mom, Layla ↘

↖ My dad, Walter

My dad, Walter, is the coolest wilderness guide
there is. People come to the Trading Post and ask
for Dad to take them on nature tours to see the
Alaskan wilderness. Sometimes I get to come, too!
My dad knows a lot about the land and animals
and loves to share his knowledge with other
people. He's also a huge
goofball. He tells the best,
most hilarious stories. Like
the one about bumping
into a baby bison—in the
dark!

Read more about
storytelling in my
family on page 28!

# Meet my Grandpa Nat!

Grandpa Nat is my mom's dad. He is a volcanologist, which means he studies volcanoes. There are over a hundred volcanoes in Alaska! Pretty cool, right? Grandpa Nat grew up on the land without electricity or running water. He knows all about respecting the land and animals and our community's traditions. My name for Grandpa is **Schada'a** (CHA-dah)—that just means grandpa in the Dena'ina language. And Grandpa calls me **Shgguya** (Suh-GOY-uh), which means my grandchild.

Read more about the languages of Alaska on pages 34–35!

My grandpa Na

# My family runs the Denali Trading Post.

The Denali Trading Post is where everyone in Qyah goes to shop for outdoor things and catch up on the latest news. It's also the first stop for scientists and explorers planning an adventure. We've got everything you need—fishing poles, bug spray, rafting tubes, and more!

My parents let me run the cash register at the Trading Post. I get to meet fun people from all over the world! But running the post means more than just selling supplies.

Next to the Trading Post is a bunkhouse that travelers can stay in. We also transport people and supplies in Mom's plane. And we keep track of what's going on all over interior Alaska. It's a full time job—which is why the Trading Post is open all year round.

# Want a tour of my room?

Basketball hoop to practice my jump shot for our team, the Qyah Northern Lights.

I hung this solar system above my bed after making it at school.

My awesome telescope that lets me see stars, solar systems, the Milky Way, and more!

I love helping my mom and dad run the Trading Post. But when I need a little peace and quiet, I head upstairs to my room. All my favorite things are here!

Look at this doll Auntie Merna hand made for me.

I keep my favorite books on this shelf.

A picture of me and Trini!

M is for Molly!

My stuffed puffin.

I keep track on my map of where visitors to the Trading Post come from. We've even had visitors from Australia!

# My Dog, Suki

Suki is the best dog in the world! She's an Alaskan Malamute. Malamutes are really strong, so they are really good at being sled dogs. Suki's favorite food is salmon skin. I met Suki on my tenth birthday. My mom and I heard some growling noises at the Trading Post and thought it was a wild beast. When my birthday cake went missing, we investigated . . . and found Suki! Even though she ate my whole birthday cake, it was love at first sight.

## PART 2

# My Community and Traditions

Fiddle music at the Fun-Raiser

Here we are at the Tribal Hall
Playing traditional music

# My Qyah Community

The population of my town, Qyah, is just 94 people—not including dogs, moose, or caribou! Qyah is north of Denali, which is the tallest mountain in North America.

A lot of interesting people come to Qyah, either to live or just to pass through. Everyone in my community is good at something, and when we have a problem we all come together to fix it. I love the people in my community—and I love meeting new people, too! Everyone's always got a fun story to share.

# Here are some of my favorite people:

## Auntie Midge

Auntie Midge is Qyah's Tribal Chief. She works with our Tribal Council to help make decisions for the Qyah community. She also uses her radio to keep everybody informed about what's going on.

## Nina

Nina is an environmental journalist. That means she writes news about what's happening in nature. Nina loves animals and plants and feels most at home in the outdoors.

## Mr. Patak

Mr. Patak owns the wood shop in town. When I was little, I thought Mr. Patak was Santa Claus, because he carved a lot of toys, like canoes and animals. He can make pretty much anything out of wood.

## Daniel

Daniel is Trini's dad and the town librarian. Daniel has sailed all over the world and even saw whales on some of his trips! He's also a fly-fisherman. Fly-fishing is sort of like regular fishing, but with different equipment.

# My Family's Traditions

My family is from the interior of Alaska. That's an area near the center of Alaska.

People with many different backgrounds live in interior Alaska, including many Alaska Native people, like my family!

An important tradition for my family and other Alaska Native families is telling stories. Stories have been passed down from family to family for thousands of years! My favorite stories are the tall tales my grandpa tells. You should hear the one about the first fish he ever caught— Grandpa said it had fangs like a saber-toothed tiger!

I couldn't wait to tell my first fish story!

Look at THIS picture I found of my grandpa Nat when he was my age playing the drum. It turns out Grandpa Nat is an amazing musician!

# Music and Dancing in My Community

Fiddle and drum music can be found at just about every celebration in my community. And where there's music . . . there's dancing! Check out Trini and me dancing Trini's first jig dance at the Tribal Hall.

Special occasions call for special music. During these times, Alaska Native people sing our Native songs, dance with friends and family, and play musical instruments like the fiddle. Sometimes we wear traditional clothes called regalia. Our regalia is made of tanned moose or caribou hide and is covered in beaded patterns. Here's me in my regalia.

# All About Beading

One of my favorite things
to do with my mom is beading.
My mom can bead ANYTHING—
from slippers to gloves and belts!

The symbols in our
beading designs
represent families
and tell stories.

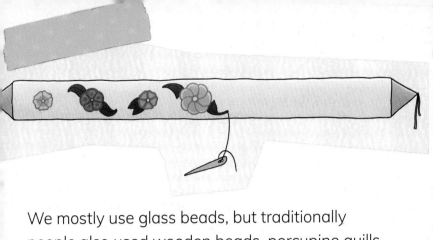

We mostly use glass beads, but traditionally people also used wooden beads, porcupine quills, seeds, and dentalia shells. People have kept this tradition going for centuries! Wearing clothing with beading feels special because it celebrates my Alaska Native heritage.

Here's a beaded picture frame I made with my mom!

# Alaska Native Languages

This is a language map of Alaska. It shows you the Native languages spoken in different parts of Alaska.

Iñupiaq

Naukan Yupik

Sirenik

Siberian Yupik

Koyukon

Holikachuk

Upper Kuskokwim

Deg Xinag

Central Yup'ik

Dena'ina

Alutiiq / Sugpiaq

Unangax

There are many different Alaska Native groups, and we have twenty officially recognized Alaska Native languages in Alaska. For example, my grandpa speaks Dena'ina and Gwich'in, and I'm learning to speak Gwich'in, too!

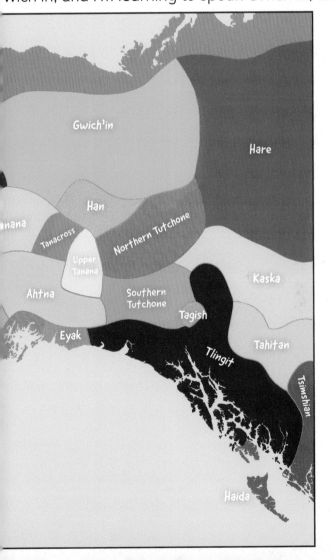

# Learn Alaska Native Words

If you're interested in Alaskan languages like me, I've written down some words that you can practice . . . in case you ever visit Alaska! And if you do, stop by the Trading Post to say **suvat**—that means "what's up?" in Iñupiaq!

# Native Names

In Alaska Native communities, Native names are very important, and they are often given to you by Elders. I think they're cool because they kind of say who you really are.

My Native name is Shahnyaa (**SHAAH-NYAH**). That means "One who informs us" in the Gwich'in language. My aunt Merna gave me this name, because I made a whole book of Native names to share with my community.

Here are the Native names of some people I know.

WHO: Layla, my mom
NAME: Dak Niighit
LANGUAGE: Gwich'in
MEANING: "She is rising up in the air" — perfect for a pilot!

WHO: Grandpa Nat
NAME: Nehtan Kon
LANGUAGE: Gwich'in
MEANING: "Lightning" — because he is quick in mind and body.

--------------

WHO: Walter, my dad
NAME: Yaade'kuh
LANGUAGE: Koyukon
MEANING: "His chin is big" — but my dad just thinks everyone else's chin is small!

WHO: Mr. Patak
NAME: Sanalguruq
LANGUAGE: Iñupiaq
MEANING: "He who is good at making things" — Mr. Patak can make anything out of wood.

--------------

WHO: Auntie Midge
NAME: Chaa Ki Hakii
LANGUAGE: Han Gwich'in
MEANING: "Auntie Big Shot Leader" — that's Auntie Midge, all right!

# PART 3

# My Adventures Outdoors!

Fishing with Dad

Aren't puffins adorable?

Tooey and me on a dog sled!

The northern lights!

# Winter in Alaska

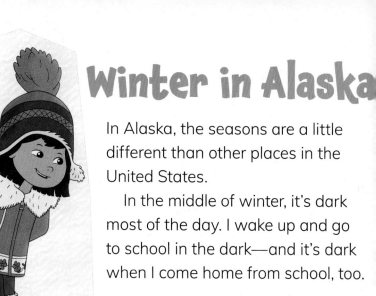

In Alaska, the seasons are a little different than other places in the United States.

In the middle of winter, it's dark most of the day. I wake up and go to school in the dark—and it's dark when I come home from school, too.

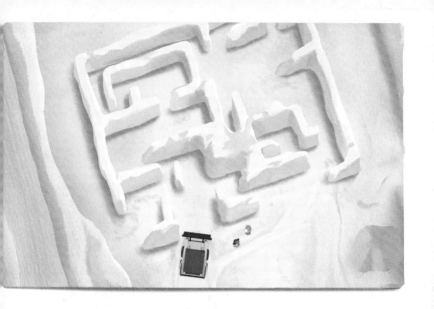

It's also so cold! Parts of Alaska can get to be 40 degrees below zero—*brrr!* We have to wear special clothing in the winter to keep us extra warm. Even though it's cold, I love the winter because there are lots of fun things to do. Above is a picture of me and Tooey and the snow maze we made. The best thing about winter is all the snow!

# Amazing Winter Activities!

You might think that because it's so cold, we don't go outside in the winter very much. But being outside is one of the best ways to enjoy winter! Here are some of my favorite things to do:

## SNOWSHOEING

When the snow gets really deep, snowshoes are a great way to get around. Snowshoes are really wide and are usually made out of bent birchwood, a cord called babiche, and heavy twine. They're built like that so you can stay on top of the snow instead of sinking into it.

## ICE FISHING

In the wintertime, rivers and lakes freeze in the cold weather—that's when it's time to go ice fishing! Ice fishing is when you make a hole in the ice of a river or lake to reach the water underneath, and you fish through that hole.

Read about summer activities on pages 50–51!

# Tooey's Sled Dogs

My MOST favorite winter activity is racing with sled
dogs. Tooey trains sled dogs with his dad, Kenji.
Dog sleds are pulled by specially trained dogs over
ice and snow. Dog sleds have been used to
transport people and supplies, and are important
to everyday life in the Arctic. They are also used
for fun! Tooey's family keeps the dogs in a kennel
outside their house.

# Here are some amazing facts about sled dogs:

1. The most common dog breeds for sled dogs are huskies and malamutes (like Suki!).

2. The person who drives the sled is called a "musher."

3. Some dog sled races are really long—up to fifteen days and over a thousand miles!

4. The most famous dog sled race is the Alaskan Iditarod Trail Sled Dog Race. Tooey's dad races in the Iditarod. Tooey wants to race in it someday!

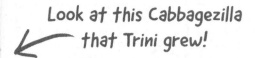

Look at this Cabbagezilla
that Trini grew!

# Summer in Alaska!

In most states in the summer, the sun can stay out for twelve hours. But in Alaska, the sun can be out for eighteen hours a day or more—and even at night, it doesn't get very dark. That's why we call it the Land of the Midnight Sun! Because of all the sunlight, veggies grow really big in the summertime.

Everyone spends a lot of time outside in the summer. Our family, and other Alaska Native families, go to fish camp! That means that as a family, we move to our camp near the river while we do our fishing. Then we smoke and dry the fish so we can have it all year round.

In our Native culture, we believe the salmon give themselves to us, and then we share our catch with family and friends.

# Amazing Summer Activities!

Here are some of my favorite things to do in the summer

## CANOEING

My ancestors used birch bark canoes, or beedoye in the Koyukon language, for transportation along our waterways. People still use canoes because they're a great way to travel on lakes and rivers! Canoes are also fun to RACE. Here's me, Tooey, and Trini practicing for a canoe race. Canoeing is all about balance, strength, teamwork, and respect for our rivers.

# HIKING and CAMPING

Whether you're outside for an afternoon hike or on an overnight adventure complete with s'mores, it's the best feeling to be connected to our traditional homelands. Be sure to wear comfy shoes and sunscreen—and don't forget bug spray!

↗ Camping with Nina, my mom, and friends

# My Favorite Thing to Do Year-Round: Bird-Watching!

| Name of Bird | Picture | Seen |
|---|---|---|
| Northern Fulmar | | ✓ |
| Northern Flicker | | ✓ |
| Belted Kingfisher | | ✓ |
| White-Crowned Sparrow | | ✓ |
| Barrows Goldeneye | | ✓ |
| Marbled Godwit | | ✓ |

I'm a BIG fan of birds. And lucky for me, Alaska is home to all sorts of birds—cranes, chickadees, puffins, and eagles, to name a few. Trini and I have seen so many, we made a chart to keep track!

# Here's how to be a thoughtful bird-watcher, like us!

1. Use the right tools. Binoculars can help you see birds up close from a safe distance. You can also use a field guide to help you identify the birds you see.

2. Practice listening. Every bird has its own unique call. It's easier to identify birds when you can see AND hear them.

3. Bring company! Bird-watching is a really fun activity, but it's even better with friends.

PYGMY OWL

Pygmy Owl is named for its small size.

puffin

53

# Getting Around in Alaska

In Alaska, getting where you're going is half the adventure!

No matter what time of year, there are lots of things to see and do in Alaska. But sometimes these amazing sights are deep into the wilderness. So how do you get there? Lots of ways!

My mom flies a bush plane to get from place to place. Bush planes are specifically meant to be flown in the wilderness. They're perfect for exploring nature!

When a raven untied our boat so it floated away down the river, Auntie Midge showed Tooey and me how to build a raft! Auntie Midge is an expert at rafting.

Tooey's dad, Kenji, has a snow machine for traveling in the snow! He spends a lot of time in the snow training sled dogs, so the snow machine helps him get around fast.

Have fun exploring Alaska—however you get where you're going!

# Animal Adventures

There are so many amazing animals in Alaska.

## Caribou

\* Caribou are called vadzaih in the Gwich'in language.

\* Once, I saw a herd of vadzaih when flying in my mom's plane over the amazing Arctic National Widlife Refuge. This herd is called the Porcupine Caribou Herd and it is very important to our people.

## Bald Eagles

\* Bald eagles are called k'eyone in the Koyukon language.

\* There are more bald eagles in Alaska than in any other state.

\* I'll never forget the time my dad and I saw two baby bald eagles hatching in their nest!

# Arctic Foxes

\* Arctic foxes are called k'ets'eeya baaye' in the Koyukon language.

\* They have thick fur coats, so they can live in temperatures of almost a hundred degrees BELOW ZERO!

\* Tooey's dog Anka met an Arctic fox once!

# Minks

\* Minks are called chihdzuu in the Gwich'in language.

\* They are cute little animals with soft fur. But when they spray, watch out—they leave a BIG smell!

\* Trini and I got sprayed by a mink once. That was one of my most hilarious moments ever!

# Alaska's Land

Alaska has some of the most amazing physical features in the world!

## Volcanoes

There are over one hundred volcanoes in Alaska! Did you know that volcanoes have a strong smell? When I went to visit my Grandpa when he was studying one, I found out volcanoes release a gas called sulfur.

# Hot springs

Where there are volcanoes, there are often hot springs nearby! Hot springs are pools of water that are heated by melted rock called magma under the Earth's surface. That's what makes the water so hot even when the weather outside is cold. I know firsthand that drinking hot chocolate in a hot spring is the best thing ever.

# The Northern Lights

The northern lights are colorful, glowing lights that appear in the sky. They can be pink, purple, green, and aqua blue, and they dance across the sky!

I'm lucky, because where I live, I can see the northern lights more often than most kids. The northern lights are easiest to see when it's a clear night, and in the winter or springtime—and usually really late at night!

The Koyukon word for the northern lights is yoyekkuyh.

You can see the northern lights from outer space!

The northern lights are also called the aurora borealis.

# Glossary

**Alaska Native:** people whose ancestors have lived in Alaska for thousands of years—like me and my family

**beedoye:** birch bark canoe (in the Koyukon language)

**bunkhouse:** a building that travelers can sleep in overnight. The Trading Post has a bunkhouse.

**bush pilot:** a person who flies planes in remote places. My mom is a bush pilot.

**chihdzuu:** mink (in the Gwich'in language)

**fish camp:** a place that Alaska Native families traditionally visit in the summertime to catch and prepare fish

**k'ets'eeyh baaye':** arctic fox (in the Koyukon language)

**k'eyone:** bald eagle (in the Koyukon language)

**Native name:** many Alaska Native people have special names given to them in their Native language. I have a Gwich'in Athabascan name.

**neet'ihthan:** I love you (in the Gwich'in language)

**regalia:** traditional clothes worn on certain occasions in Alaska Native culture

**schada'a:** grandpa (in the Dena'ina language)

**shida:** my friend (in the Dena'ina language)

**shgguya:** grandchild (in the Dena'ina language)

**suvat:** what's up (in the Iñupiaq language)

**teekkone:** wolf (in the Koyukon language)

**tradition:** an important belief or behavior in your culture that has been followed for a long time

**vadzaih:** caribou (in the Gwich'in language)

**volcanologist:** a scientist who studies volcanoes, like my grandpa

**yoyekkuyh:** northern lights (in the Koyukon language)

# Thanks for reading!

I hope you liked learning about my amazing family and friends, our unique community and traditions, and all the awesome ways we get to enjoy the outdoors up here in Alaska. Maybe you could come visit sometime and go on some adventures of your own!

Your friend,
Molly

## Mahsi'choo!

Thank you in Gwich'in